What's in Your Bag?

by Mrs. Moore's and
Mrs. Rapauno's classes
with Tony Stead

capstone

What is a habitat? A habitat is a place where animals and plants live.

We thought about habitats we would like to visit. Then we wrote about where we would go and described what we would see and feel. Most important, we talked about what to pack for a visit.

Mountains

by Joshua and Nicholas

The mountains are filled with trees and bushes. There are caves, too. Bears, mountain lions, snow leopards, and mountain goats live in the mountains.

It is breezy, sometimes cold, and sometimes snowy in the mountains.

What You Would Take:

- a lot of gear
- water
- a coat
- food

Forests

by Spencer

Lots of rabbits, wolves, squirrels, and frogs live in the forest habitat. There are also lots of plants like ivy and shrubs.

In the spring flowers bloom and trees grow. During summer it can be green with lots of life. The leaves turn brown, red, yellow, and orange during autumn. In winter the trees and bushes are bare.

What You Would Take:

- bug spray
- spare clothes
- sneakers
- shorts

Arctic Life

by Bryan

In the arctic you will see ice, polar bears, and icy ponds. The weather at the arctic is cold in the winter and cool during the summer.

You can find this habitat in the northern parts of the world.

What You Would Take:

- a coat
- gloves
- a hat
- food
- a sled

Swamps

by Alexander

If you visit a swamp, you will see frogs, fish, and alligators. It looks like mush with mud, water, and rocks. The swamp is warm, wet, and sunny.

What You Would Take:

- boots
- a net
- water

Rain Forests

by Madison and Layla

The rain forest is hot and rainy. Toucans and spiders live in the rain forest. Gorillas, chimpanzees, and parrots also live there. This habitat is filled with trees, plants, and vines.

What You Would Take:

- bug spray
- a hat
- an umbrella
- granola bars
- a flashlight
- heavy shoes

Deserts

by A'Kai and Taija

Deserts are very hot and sunny. In the desert, you will see scorpions, owls, cacti, lizards, and camels.

What You Would Take:

- water
- sunglasses
- a book bag for gear

camale
lizard
owl

Our classes talked a lot about the places we could visit and what each would look like. Lots of us had a favorite habitat we would want to visit. Which one would you want to visit? What would you bring?